SUPER HEROES

BATGIRL ™

AND THE QUEEN OF GREEN

WRITTEN BY
LAURIE S. SUTTON

ILLUSTRATED BY
LEONEL CASTELLANI

BASED ON CHARACTERS CREATED BY
BOB KANE WITH BILL FINGER

STONE ARCH BOOKS
a capstone imprint

Published by Stone Arch Books, an imprint of Capstone.
1710 Roe Crest Drive
North Mankato, Minnesota 56003
www.capstonepub.com

Library of Congress Cataloging-in-Publication Data
Names: Sutton, Laurie S., author. | Castellani, Leonel, illustrator.
Title: Batgirl and the Queen of Green / by Laurie S. Sutton ; illustrated by Leonel
    Castellani.
Description: North Mankato, Minnesota : Stone Arch Books, an imprint of Capstone,
    [2021] | Series: DC super hero adventures | Based on characters created by Bob
    Kane with Bill Finger. | Audience: Ages 8-11. | Audience: Grades 4-6. | Summary:
    "Poison Ivy wants to protect the plants in Gotham City Park from climate change.
    Although that may sound like a noble plan, her solution actually seals off the
    entire park inside a giant, plant-based dome! With helpless citizens trapped inside,
    it's up to Batgirl to fight through the villain's fearsome flora"—Provided by
    publisher.
Identifiers: LCCN 2020027080 (print) | LCCN 2020027081 (ebook) | ISBN
    9781515882138 (library binding) | ISBN 9781515883227 (paperback) | ISBN
    9781515891772 (pdf)
Subjects: CYAC: Superheroes—Fiction. | Supervillains—Fiction. | Plants—Fiction
Classification: LCC PZ7.S968294 Bam 2021 (print) | LCC PZ7.S968294 (ebook) | DDC
    [Fic]—dc23
LC record available at https://lccn.loc.gov/2020027080
LC ebook record available at https://lccn.loc.gov/2020027081

Designer: Hilary Wacholz

TABLE OF CONTENTS

Growing up in Gotham City, Barbara Gordon often saw Batman bring justice to those who needed it most. But when her father, Police Commissioner James Gordon, was arrested for a crime he didn't commit, she couldn't sit back and hope for a hero. Donning a Batsuit of her own design, she set out to clear her father's name without his knowledge. With her brilliant mind and a mastery of martial arts, Barbara did more than simply free her father. She also earned a permanent place in the Batman Family.

She became . . .

BATGIRL™

CHAPTER 1

Poison Paradise

The sun was starting to rise on a new day in Gotham City. Batgirl had been on patrol all night long, making sure that the people of Gotham City were safe. As she turned her Batcycle toward home, she heard a police alert on the radio in her helmet.

WOOP! WOOP! WOOP!

"All units! Respond to an emergency in Gotham City Park!" the voice said.

Batgirl revved her Batcycle and sped down the street. There wasn't much traffic this early in the morning, and she was able to arrive very quickly. As she cruised around the edge of the park, she was amazed by what she saw!

A huge wall of thick, woody vines was sprouting up out of the ground and starting to surround the park. The vines grew to enormous size in moments, waving like the tentacles of a monster squid.

Not only were the vines gigantic, they had weird growths all over them. They were covered in what looked like huge Venus flytrap pods, sharp thorns, and barbs. Some of the vines reached out and whipped at a group of police vehicles that had arrived on the scene.

WHIIIP! WHIIIP!

These plants aren't natural, Batgirl thought. *Mother Nature didn't make them. But I can guess who did.*

Batgirl rode her Batcycle along the outside of the wall. She soon saw a woman dressed in a bright-green costume waving her arms the same way the vines were waving. She was controlling the plants. Batgirl recognized the woman right away.

"Poison Ivy!" Batgirl said. "What is she up to now?"

Batgirl was about to go get answers from the super-villain when she heard a call for help. She turned and saw a police officer in the grip of one of the Venus flytrap pods. The monster plant was closing up around him like a clam.

"Help! Get me out of this thing!" the cop yelled.

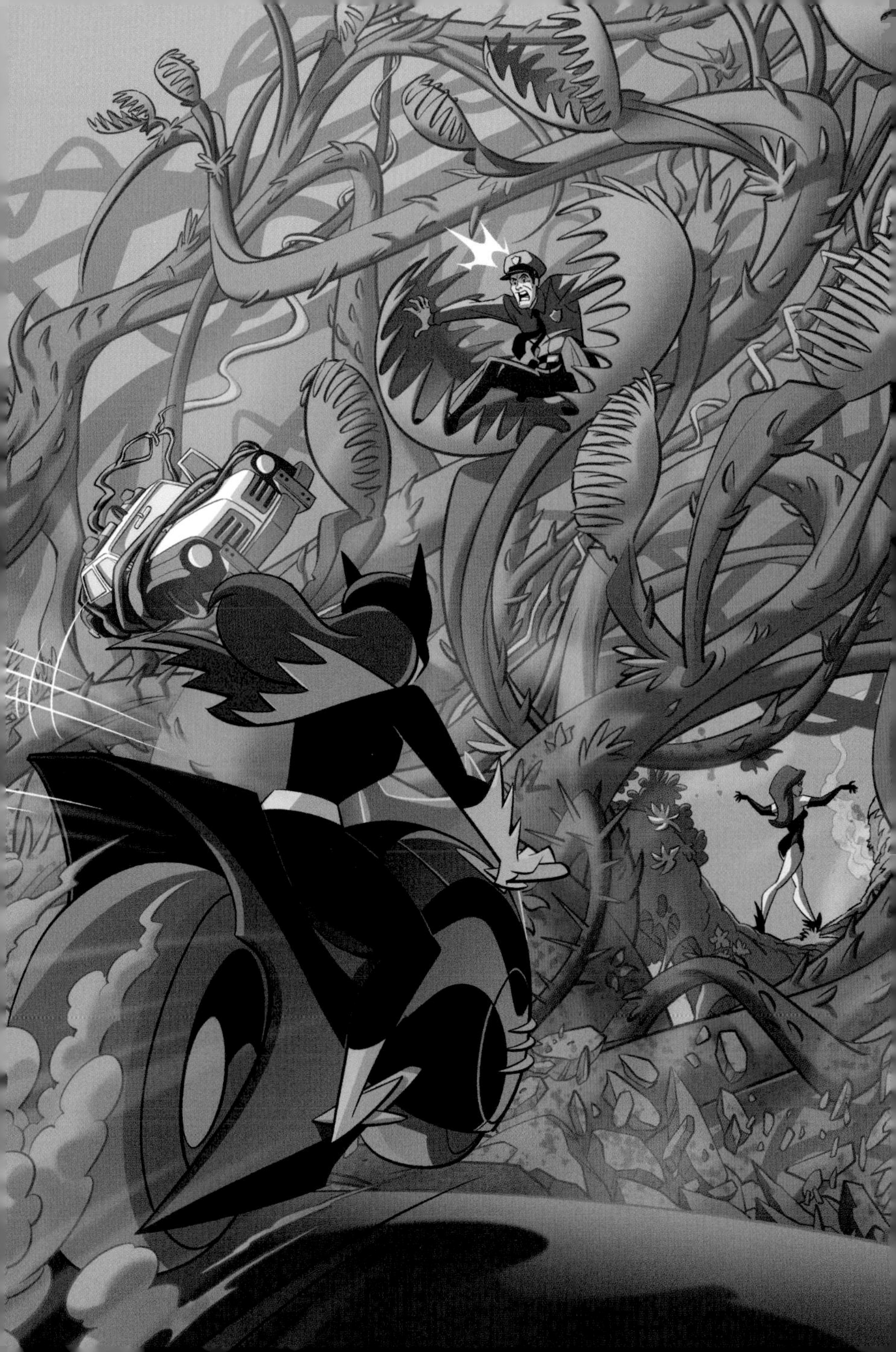

VROOOOM!

Batgirl zoomed toward the struggling police officer. Her movement made the other Venus flytraps turn toward her as she passed them. The pods opened and closed like hungry mouths.

When she reached the trapped officer, Batgirl jumped off her Batcycle. She let the bike keep going forward to attract the mutant flytrap pods. As they turned to follow the movement of the Batcycle, Batgirl took a grapnel from her Utility Belt and launched it toward the pod holding the cop.

KTHUUUNK!

The grapnel latched onto the bottom half of the pod. Batgirl pulled on the Batrope attached to the grapnel with all her strength. The pod opened just enough for the officer to crawl out.

"Thanks, Batgirl!" the officer gasped. "For a minute there, I thought I was a goner."

Paramedics ran up to help the rescued officer. Gotham City Police Commissioner Gordon was with them.

"Batgirl, Poison Ivy is creating a wall of plants around the entire park," he said. "We don't know why she's doing this, but there are people still inside the park. They'll be trapped."

"Then I better stop Poison Ivy before that happens," Batgirl said.

Batgirl saw that the wall was not complete yet. Poison Ivy stood in a big, open space. But the police could not get anywhere near the super-villain. The huge vines cracked like whips to protect her.

SNAAAP! SNAAAP!

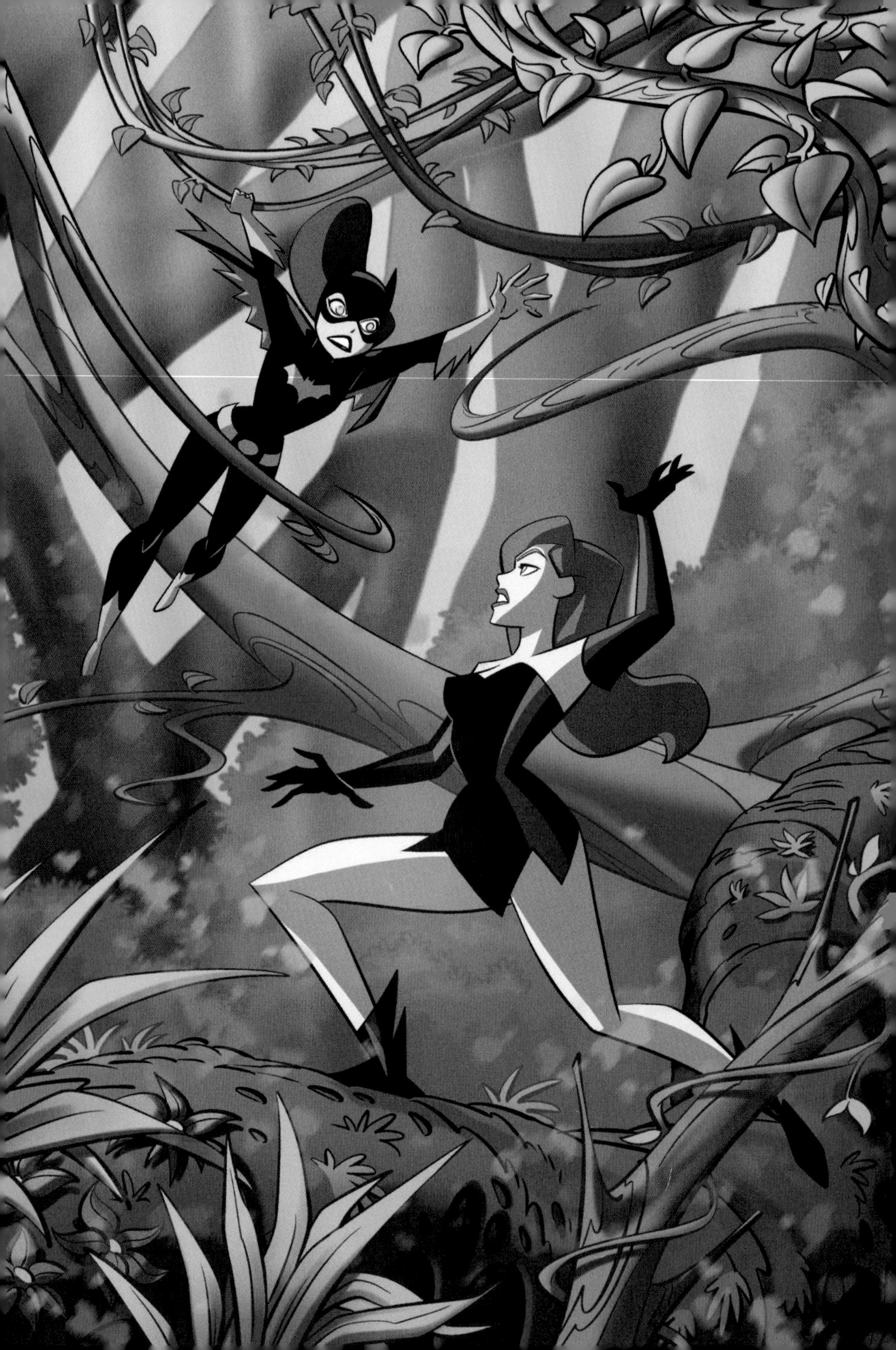

Batgirl ran toward the twisting tendrils. They reached out to grab her, but the hero dodged their grasp. She spun in a cartwheel between two grasping vines and then used another vine to lift her over the rest. Batgirl swung from vine to vine like a kid on a set of monkey bars. She had almost reached Poison Ivy when a giant tendril caught her from behind.

"Uhhh!" Batgirl gasped as the vine tightened around her body.

Poison Ivy gestured and the plant brought Batgirl over to her.

"Batgirl! I won't let you ruin my special project," Poison Ivy said.

"Your project is putting people in danger," Batgirl said. "I've already had to rescue a police officer from one of your plants."

"That's nothing compared to what people have done to plants," Ivy replied angrily. "Because of humans, the planet has warmed up. The climate is out of balance. The plants are suffering."

Batgirl knew that Poison Ivy had a passion for plants. She had been a botanist before she became a super-villain.

"Is that what this is about? Are you taking revenge on the humans of Gotham City?" Batgirl asked.

"I don't care about people," Ivy replied. "I am the Queen of Green. My goal is to protect plants. My special vines are going to weave a dome over Gotham City Park. All the trees and flowers and grass inside will be protected from the climate catastrophe that is coming."

"But there are still people in the park," Batgirl said.

"I will deal with them when the dome is complete," Ivy replied.

Batgirl looked up at the giant vines that were curving overhead like an upside-down bowl. Bright beams of sunlight poured down through the woven vines and into the park. The dome still had a large opening at the very top.

Poison Ivy gestured and the vine holding Batgirl stretched out and away from the villain. Another vine grabbed Batgirl and carried her through the tangle of the living wall. She was passed from vine to vine until she was outside of the wall. The last vine dropped Batgirl next to Commissioner Gordon.

"I'm getting police reports that the wall is all the way around the park now," Gordon told her.

"And it's growing taller every minute," Batgirl said. "Ivy is making what she thinks is a safe place for plants."

"Well, it won't be a safe place for people if Poison Ivy has her way," Gordon said. "Early morning walkers and park employees are still in there."

"Ivy might think she's doing the right thing, but she's doing it the wrong way," Batgirl said. "I have to get back inside and stop her before the dome closes up for good."

CHAPTER 2

Natural Defenses

Batgirl studied the ever-growing dome of mutant vines, searching for a way to get through them. They were as thick as tree trunks where they grew out of the ground. But as the vines grew higher, they got thinner. They twined together wildly, but loosely, like an open basket weave.

"Hmmm. Ivy left gaps in the dome for sunlight and rain to get in," Batgirl observed. "That means I can get in."

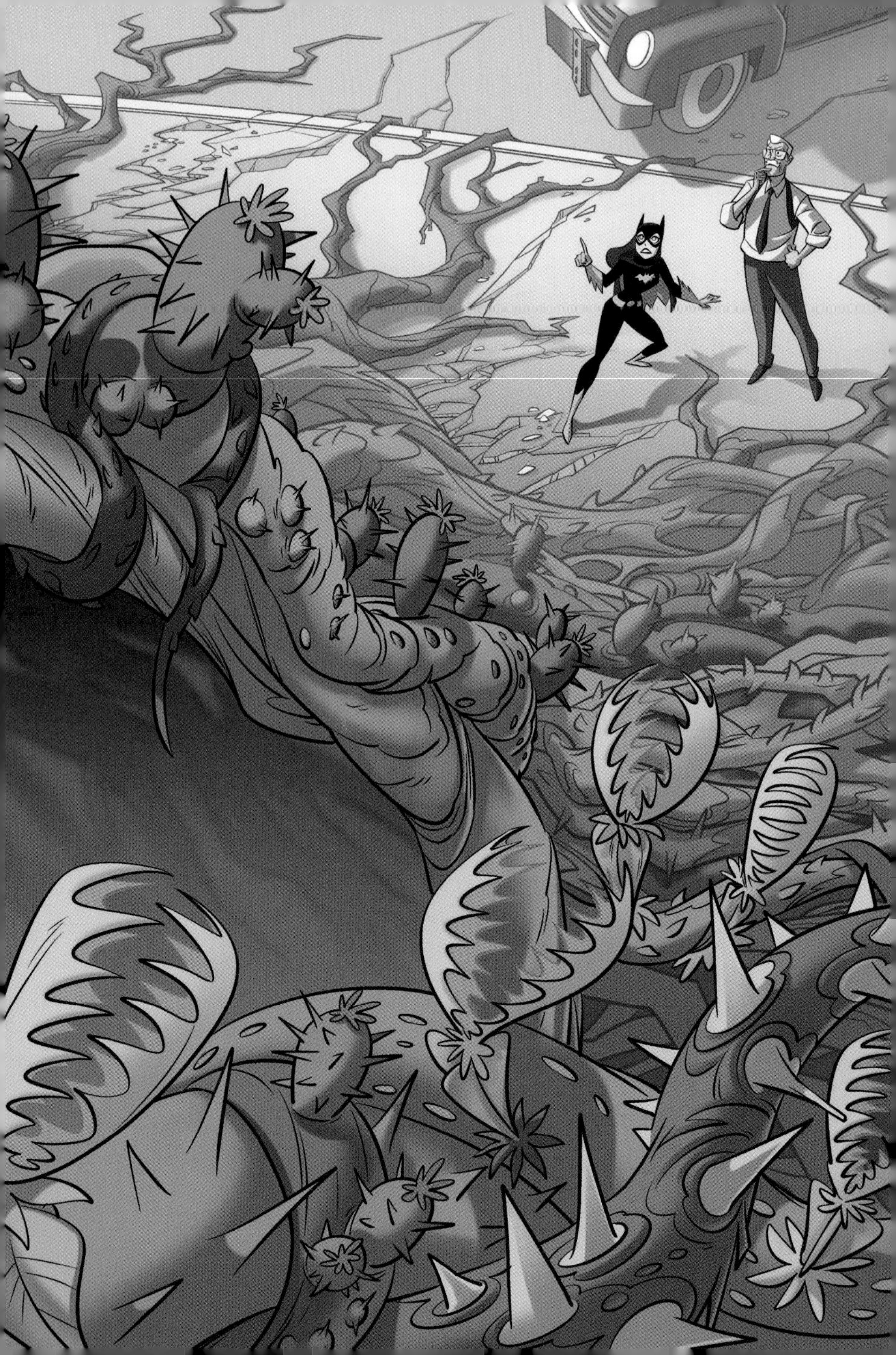

"But where exactly?" Commissioner Gordon asked.

"There," Batgirl said. She pointed to a medium-sized opening sixty feet above where they stood.

A few more gaps appeared, but they were even higher up on the mutant wall. As Batgirl and Gordon watched, the openings stretched and shrank, becoming larger and smaller as the dome evolved.

"I don't know," Gordon said, rubbing his chin. "That looks . . . dangerous."

"All I have to do is climb past all the Venus flytrap pods, cactus spines, and giant thorns growing on the vines," Batgirl said. Then she pointed even higher up the dome. "My only other choice is to drop down into the opening at the very top of the dome before it closes."

"I can have a police helicopter here in twenty minutes," Commissioner Gordon said.

"We don't have time to wait for it," Batgirl said. "The dome might be completely sealed off before then."

Batgirl pulled a grapnel from her Utility Belt and aimed it at a spot near the gap in the mutant wall.

"I can use this to get past some of the wall's defenses, but then I have to climb the rest of the way," Batgirl said. "Wish me luck."

She did not wait for Commissioner Gordon to reply.

FWOOOSH! THUNK!

Batgirl fired the grapnel and it sank into the bark of one of the thick vines.

SHUDDDERRR! The vine shook in response.

As Batgirl swung up on her Batrope, the nearby gap squeezed shut.

Oh great. Ivy is not going to make this easy, Batgirl thought.

A group of Venus flytrap pods turned toward Batgirl and opened their mouths as soon as her feet landed on the surface of the vine wall. There was a thick, sweet smell coming from the plants. It was like cotton candy and peppermint and chocolate all rolled into one delicious scent. Batgirl was tempted to lean toward the plant and sniff it like a flower.

No. It's a lure, Batgirl realized. *The police officer I rescued must have been drawn in by it and was caught.*

Then the pods pulsed slightly and the sweet smell got even more intense.

Ugh. It's as if the flytraps can sense that their prey isn't taking their bait. And I'm their prey, Batgirl thought. *The scent is starting to make me feel dizzy.*

Batgirl reached into her Utility Belt and pulled out a small oxygen mask. She strapped it over her nose and mouth. After a few deep breaths, she felt better.

I have to get past these flytraps and climb up to the next gap, Batgirl decided. *Hmm. If they want to "eat" I guess I'll have to "feed" them—sort of like giving the guard dog a bone to chew on.*

Batgirl opened a compartment in her Utility Belt. She pulled out a few small smoke-screen canisters and tossed them into the open mouths of the pods.

SNAAAP! SNAAAP! The flytraps closed up around the canisters.

Just as I thought, the plants react to anything going into their mouths. It doesn't have to be a person, Batgirl observed.

Batgirl leaped up onto the closed pods and used them like living stepping-stones to climb higher on the wall of giant vines. She left the Venus flytraps behind her, but soon she faced a different mutant threat.

WOOOOSH!

A cactus spine the size of an Olympic javelin zoomed past Batgirl from above. Her well-trained reflexes saved her. She twisted out of the way just in time, but she lost her balance and fell off the wall!

Batgirl was not afraid. She was frustrated at losing all her progress as she fell past the Venus flytraps, but she was not frightened. She knew her physical skills and the contents of her Utility Belt would save her.

Batgirl grabbed a grapnel from her belt. Taking careful aim, she fired it at the wall of mutant vines.

SHTHUUUUNK!

The grapnel gripped the thick bark and the Batrope attached to it snapped tight. Batgirl used the momentum from her fall to swing back up in a smooth arc. As she zoomed even higher up the wall of vines, the hero spotted the perfect place to land.

Unfortunately, Batgirl never got the chance. Clumps of mutant cactus pods suddenly sprouted out of the vine trunk she was aiming for. All the spines on the pods turned toward her.

WOOOSH! WOOOSH!

A volley of huge spikes shot out at the super hero.

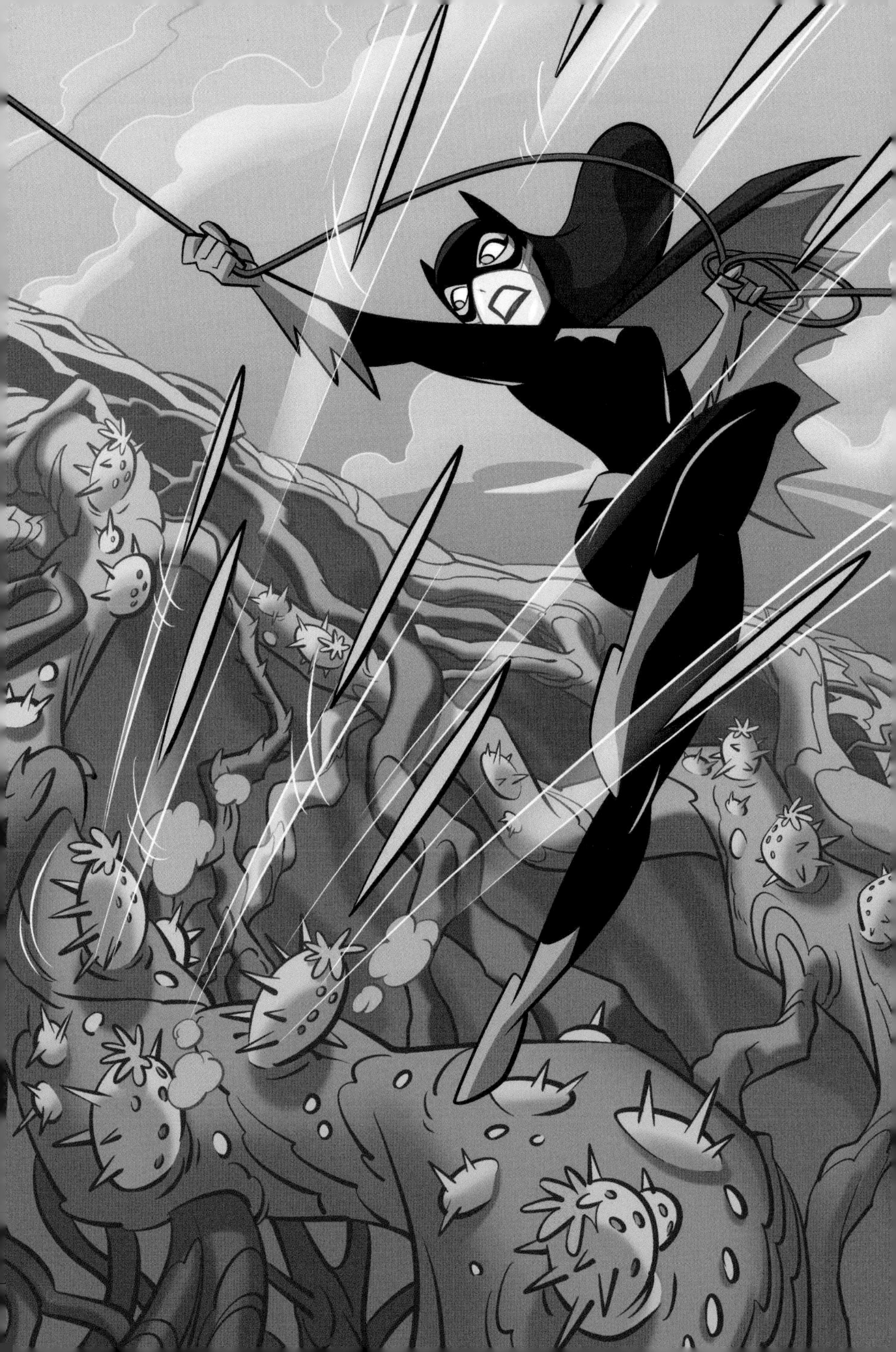

Batgirl twisted on the end of her Batrope to dodge the dangerous spines. She used her amazing acrobatic skills, making her look like she was dancing in midair. All the spines missed her.

Batgirl reached the end of her swing. She shifted her weight and balance to get ready for the return swing and landing. And then she heard an unfortunate sound.

SNIIICK!

A final cactus spike shot out from the wall and hit the Batrope. The rope vibrated and Batgirl felt its fibers begin to separate.

SNAP! The rope gave way and the hero was falling. Again.

I'm down to my last grapnel, Batgirl realized as she reached into her Utility Belt.

THWUP! THWUP! THWUP!

Batgirl heard the sound of a helicopter. It swooped toward the hero like a bird of prey. The pilot tipped the aircraft on its side just in time to scoop up Batgirl in the middle of her fall.

THUUUD!

Batgirl landed in the open passenger cabin in the back of the chopper.

"Welcome aboard, Batgirl," the pilot shouted over the noise of the helicopter engines. A moment later the aircraft returned to level flying.

"Owww, thanks," Batgirl shouted back as she shoved aside her oxygen mask. She rubbed her bruised ribs from the hard fall into the cabin. "And thanks to Commissioner Gordon for sending a police helicopter. You were fast. He said no one could get here in less than twenty minutes."

"Well, he wasn't talking about *me*," the pilot replied.

"I think the police commissioner will be talking about you after this," Batgirl promised. "Now, let's get to the top of this dome. I need to get inside and put a stop to Poison Ivy's plan."

Face·to·Face

Batgirl climbed into the copilot's seat of the police helicopter.

"What's your name?" she asked the pilot.

"Lieutenant Susan Brighthawk, at your service," the woman replied.

"You have the perfect name for your profession," Batgirl said with a smile.

"So do you," Lieutenant Brighthawk said, grinning back.

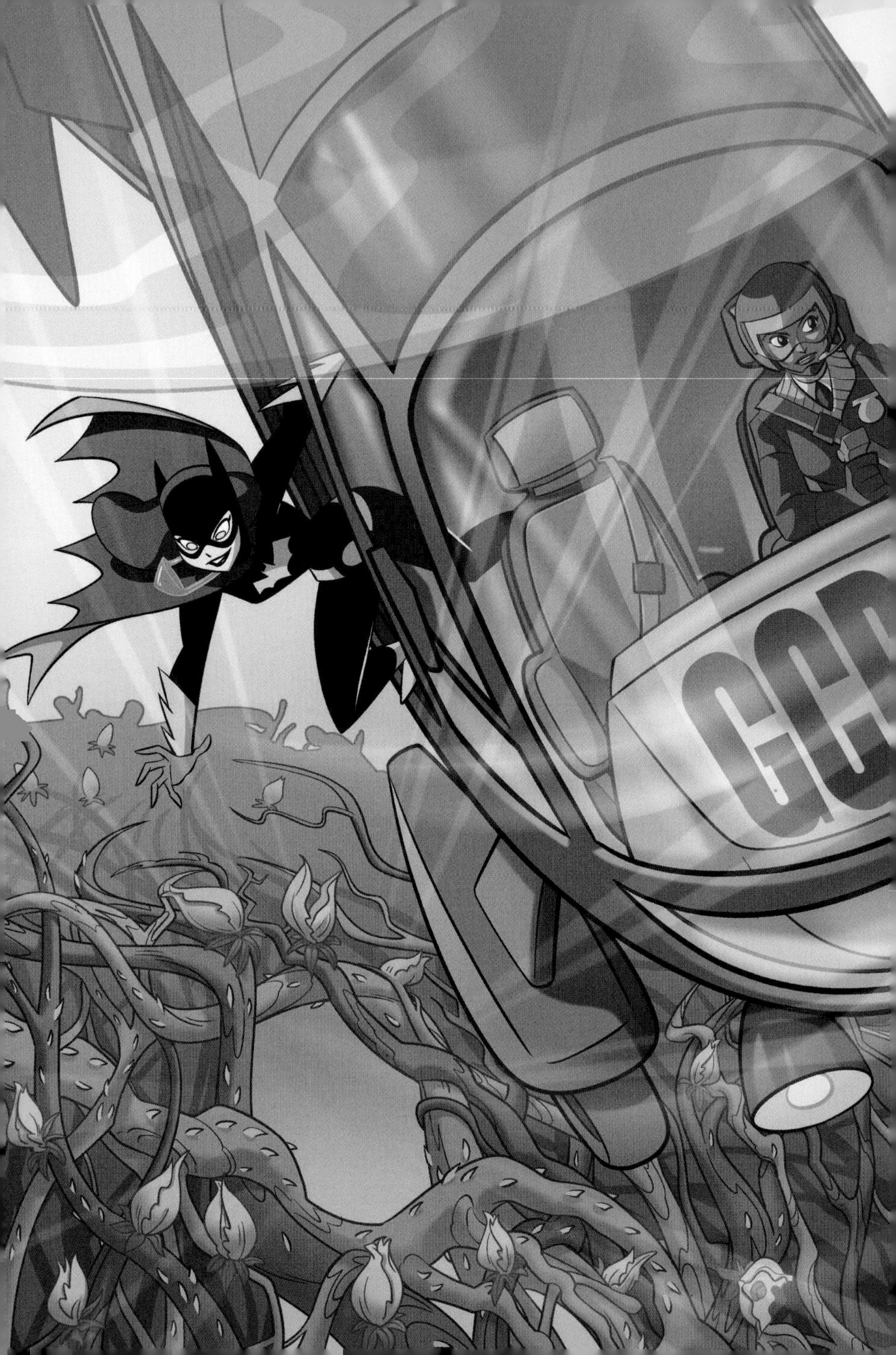

The pilot banked her aircraft above the growing vine dome. This was the first time Batgirl had been able to get a good look at the whole structure. It took up several city blocks and was many stories high. The entire park was surrounded.

"The dome is closing fast," Batgirl said. She pointed to the vines reaching toward each other at the top. "I have to get down there before it's too late."

"Hold on to your cape," Lieutenant Brighthawk said just before she put the helicopter into a steep dive.

Suddenly, fresh new vines grew out of the dome and lunged toward the aircraft. Clumps of giant cactus spines sprouted out of the ends of the vines and shot their quills at the helicopter. Lieutenant Brighthawk turned her aircraft into a steep bank.

THUP! THUP! THUP!

The rotor blades dug into the air and hauled the helicopter out of harm's way. Lieutenant Brighthawk looked over at the copilot's seat to see if Batgirl was all right, but the cockpit door was open and the seat was empty.

"Oh no! She fell out!" the pilot gasped.

Then Lieutenant Brighthawk saw Batgirl sliding and swinging down the new vine shoots. She was using them as a path to get to the opening in the dome.

"Wow! That Batgirl has some serious skills," Lieutenant Brighthawk shouted.

Batgirl leaped over the last clump of sprouting spikes and sprinted toward the opening in the dome. She pulled her last grapnel from her Utility Belt.

All I need is a single anchor point and I can swing down into the park, Batgirl thought as she took aim.

But then she saw something that made her stop.

Poison Ivy rose up on a platform of plants in front of Batgirl. It was made of flowers and tender new growth that almost glowed in the bright morning sun. These plants were completely different from the hard vines and other dangerous flora that made the dome.

"Batgirl. You just don't give up," the super-villain said. "Go away. I'm trying to do something *good* here."

"We don't have the same definition of 'good,' Ivy," Batgirl replied. "You could be using your powers to help with reforestation or growing crops in deserts."

Batgirl quickly threw a Batarang at her foe. The weapon whizzed past Poison Ivy and went wide of its target.

"Ha ha ha!" Poison Ivy laughed. "You missed!"

The Batarang made a wide curve through the air like a boomerang. It swooped back toward the super-villain and struck her from behind.

THHHONK!

"Looks like I didn't," Batgirl said as she ran toward the dazed villain.

Poison Ivy fell to her knees. She was down but not defeated. She waved her arms and a new batch of mutant flowers bloomed on the platform next to her. Ivy plucked a handful of them and threw them at Batgirl.

PWOOF! PWOOF!

The flowers burst into a big cloud of stinky pollen. The flower bombs smelled like rotting fish and sweaty socks. Batgirl started coughing and her eyes filled with tears.

"How do you like my corpse flower bombs?" Ivy asked. "They have one of the strongest odors in the plant kingdom."

The stench was incredible. Batgirl quickly pulled her oxygen mask back over her nose and mouth. Even though she could barely see through her watering eyes and the pollen cloud, Batgirl did not stop trying to get to Poison Ivy.

"All I have to say is that you shouldn't go into the perfume business," Batgirl said.

"Never! It's a horrible industry that crushes flowers!" Poison Ivy replied. "Millions of innocent plants are destroyed just so people can smell nice."

Good, keep talking, Ivy. I can't see you clearly, but I can follow the sound of your voice, Batgirl thought.

Batgirl inched her way through the smelly pollen cloud one small step at a time. She could hear Poison Ivy making her angry speech not far away.

I'm close now, Batgirl thought. She poised to leap at the blurry shape that was her foe.

Suddenly a vine reached out and grabbed Batgirl. It twined around her torso and lifted her off her feet. Her arms were pinned tightly to her sides. She could not reach her Utility Belt. Poison Ivy waved the vine over to her so that she could confront Batgirl face-to-face.

"Nice try, Batgirl," Ivy said. "But I saw you coming."

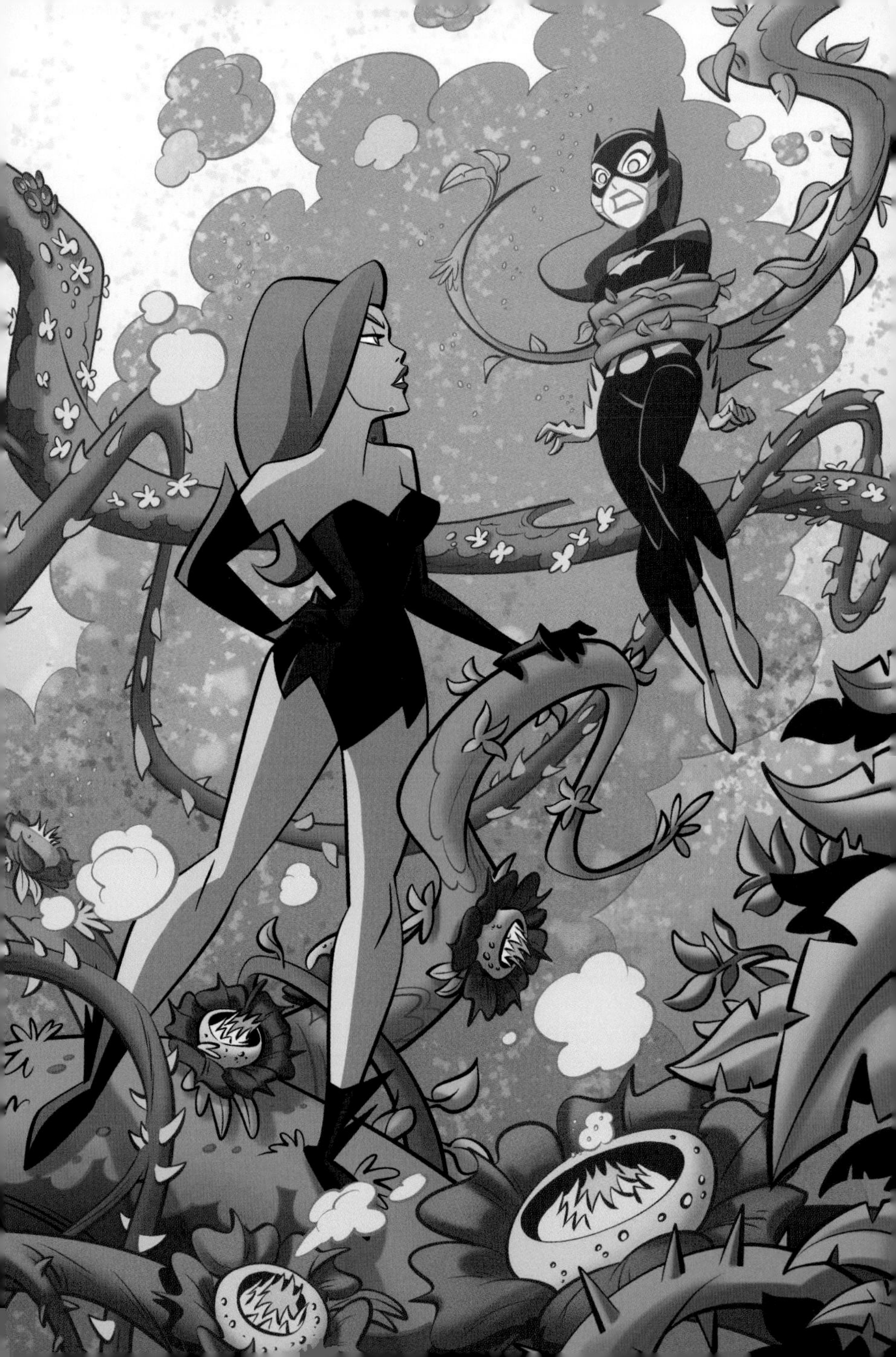

"But you didn't see *this* coming," Batgirl replied.

Batgirl used her strength and acrobatic skills to twist her body within the grip of Poison Ivy's mutant vine. She clamped her legs around the super-villain's head and neck. Poison Ivy gasped in surprise. She also gasped for breath.

"Let . . . me . . . go," Poison Ivy said.

The vines tightened around Batgirl.

Batgirl's legs tightened around Poison Ivy.

"Let *me* go," Batgirl replied.

The two foes stared each other in the eyes. Neither looked ready to give up.

Suddenly the platform started to drop. Batgirl was pulled down into the park along with Poison Ivy. The dome closed above them.

"You wanted to get in," Ivy hissed at Batgirl. "Well, now you're in."

WHAM!

The platform hit the ground like a falling tree. The impact broke Batgirl's grip on Poison Ivy and loosened the vines holding her. It also stunned the super hero. When Batgirl regained her senses, the super-villain was gone.

Batgirl got to her feet and put away her oxygen mask. When she looked at her surroundings, it seemed like everything was more green than normal. Even the air had an emerald tint. The gaps in the dome above her head let in streamers of bright, golden sunlight. Batgirl felt as if she were inside an old church with stained-glass windows.

"It's beautiful in here," Batgirl admitted. "But it's for all the wrong reasons."

Batgirl went looking for Poison Ivy. She did not get far before shouts for help attracted her attention.

Oh no. That's probably the walkers and workers Commissioner Gordon said were trapped inside the park, Batgirl thought. *They sound scared. I have to go help them. My search for Ivy will have to wait.*

CHAPTER 4

Mutant Menaces

HELP! HELP!

Batgirl ran along one of the park paths in the direction of the yelling. A few moments later she saw a group of people being threatened by a giant monster. It was made out of vines and branches and looked like a massive centipede. The people were trying to get into the shelter of the park's Visitor Center, but the beast blocked their way.

Batgirl was amazed at the sight of the plant creature. She had seen many strange things as a super hero, but this was something diffcrent!

The beast crawled on dozens of legs made out of thick tree branches and its body was woven from long vines. The monster was completely hollow on the inside. Batgirl could see straight through it.

Poison Ivy must have created guards for her private plant kingdom, Batgirl realized as she pondered her next move. *She said she'd "deal with" whoever got caught inside the dome. Now I see how she plans to do that. And I'm going to stop her.*

Batgirl ran toward the plant creature. She could not tell if it saw her. Its attention seemed to be focused only on the group of humans.

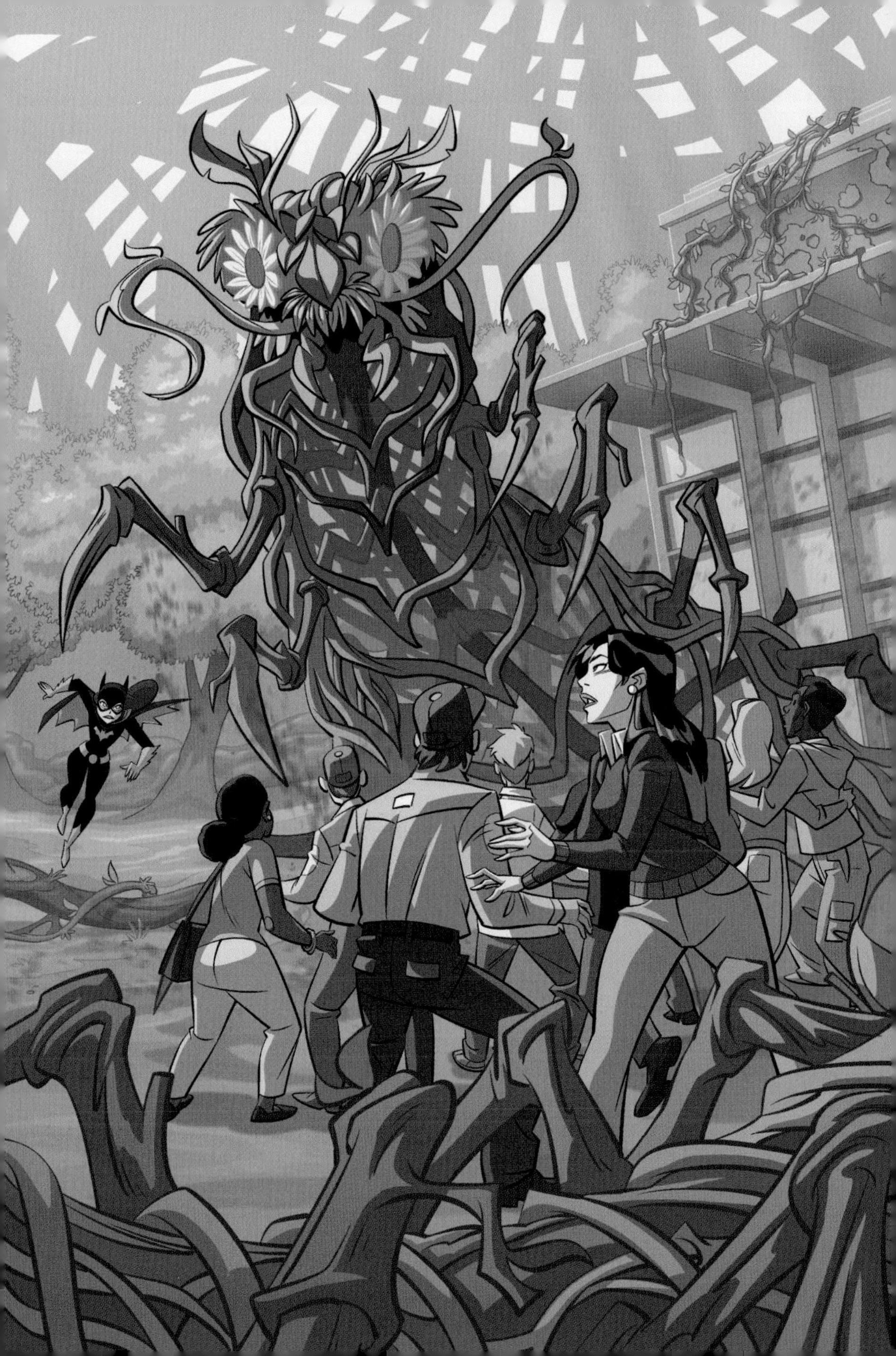

Batgirl scrambled hand-over-hand up the creature's vines and branches. Then she took a Batrope from her Utility Belt and twirled it like a lasso. The loop dropped down over the creature's head like a bridle on a horse.

"Giddyup," said Batgirl, pulling on the Batrope as if it were a set of reins.

The beast reared up on its multiple branchlike legs and then turned away from the group of people on the ground. As Batgirl guided the creature down the pathway, she watched the people scramble into the Visitor Center for safety.

After a little while, Batgirl unwrapped the Batrope from the monster's head and jumped to the ground. The beast kept plodding in the direction it was going. It did not return to threaten the people in the Visitor Center. They were safe.

Now I have to find Poison Ivy and put an end to her scheme, Batgirl thought.

STOMP! STOMP! STOMP!

Suddenly another giant plant monster came down the path toward Batgirl. This one looked like a huge T-rex made of stupendous sunflowers laced together. But when it opened its jaws, its mouth was lined with rows of big thorns for teeth. Large barbs stuck out from its tail.

Poison Ivy rode on its back.

"You are a pesky pest in my perfect plant realm," Ivy told her foe. "It's time to get rid of you."

The super-villain gestured with one hand and the plant creature whipped its long tail at Batgirl. Sharp barbs shot out toward the super hero.

WHOOOSH! WHOOOSH!

Batgirl used her acrobatic skills to twist and jump out of the way just in time. She was not harmed, but her cape was ripped to shreds.

"Hey! That was my favorite cape," Batgirl said.

Batgirl grabbed several small pellets of knockout gas from her Utility Belt and threw them at the super-villain. The pellets hit Poison Ivy right on target.

FWOOSH!

A cloud of bright-blue gas spread around the villain. But when the cloud cleared, Poison Ivy was still awake.

"Have you forgotten? I'm immune to all poisons," Ivy said with a laugh. "A little knockout gas won't work on me."

Poison Ivy waved her hand to command her plant creature to snap at Batgirl with its thorny teeth.

CHOMPPP! CHOMPPP!

Batgirl stood her ground in the face of the threat. As soon as the monster's mouth got close enough, she threw her Batrope around its muzzle.

YANK!

The hero tightened the rope and the monster's mouth clamped shut. Then Batgirl pulled the creature's head down toward her. The whole T-rex tipped forward, off-balance. It was big, but it was lightweight. It was only made of sunflowers, after all.

"Whaaat?" Poison Ivy shouted in surprise as she lurched forward. She almost fell off the creature's back.

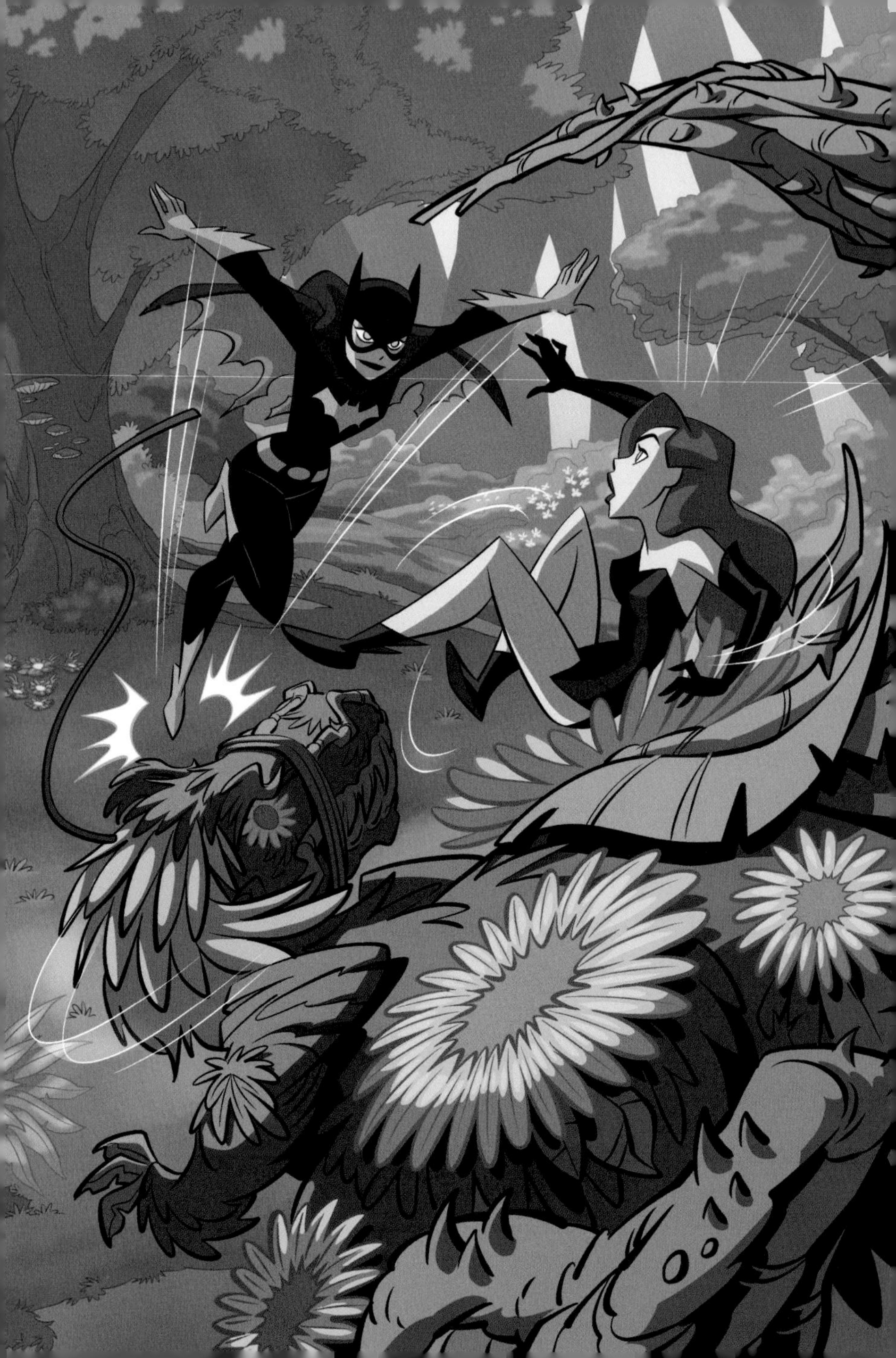

Batgirl leaped up onto the monster's muzzle and ran up the front of its face toward Poison Ivy. She did not need anything from her Utility Belt this time.

WHAM! Batgirl tackled Poison Ivy and grappled with her on the back of the giant plant creature.

Batgirl held Poison Ivy in a wrestling headlock. Then she used a leg swipe to knock the villain's legs out from under her. Poison Ivy fell face-first onto one of the giant sunflowers that formed the creature. The impact made a cloud of pollen rise up out of the sunflower like dust from an old rug.

"Achooo!" Batgirl sneezed. She could not help herself. Her eyes started to water again.

"So, you're allergic to my lovely flowers," Poison Ivy said. Suddenly all the sunflowers on the plant creature erupted with pollen.

Batgirl had her hands full fighting Poison Ivy. She could not let go of the villain to reach the oxygen mask in her Utility Belt. Batgirl tried to hold her breath and keep Poison Ivy pinned at the same time. She almost succeeded.

Poison Ivy twisted like one of her own vines and squirmed out of Batgirl's grip. Then she kicked Batgirl off the back of the plant monster.

"That does it," Poison Ivy said. "I'm going to stomp you!"

She commanded the T-rex to pound the ground where Batgirl had fallen. But when Poison Ivy looked down for her foe, there was no sign of the super hero.

"Ha! She must have run away!" Poison Ivy decided. "Now I can finish my garden in peace."

Poison Ivy rode on top of her plant creature as it lumbered away. She did not know that Batgirl was clinging to the belly of the beast.

Batgirl let Poison Ivy's plant monster secretly carry her to the super-villain's stronghold. It turned out to be more like a Garden of Eden than a fortress. The walls were made of rows of large fruit trees. The floor was covered by a thick carpet of soft green moss. Flowering vines dripped from a tall, vaulted ceiling.

Batgirl silently slipped off the plant creature and hid in the lush growth to plan her next move. She watched the T-rex carry the villain into the heart of her secret garden. Then the sunflower monster slowly came apart and sank back into the ground. Poison Ivy was gently lowered onto the soft moss.

Ivy waved her hands. A throne of blossoms and buds grew up out of the soil. Ivy plucked a pear from one of the trees and nibbled the juicy fruit. She stretched out on the leafy throne.

"I am the Queen of Green," Ivy declared. "My realm is secure."

CHAPTER 5

A Queen Dethroned

She doesn't know I'm here and feels totally safe, Batgirl thought as she watched Ivy on her throne. *Now is my chance to strike while her guard is down.*

Batgirl reached into her Utility Belt for a stun grenade. It would knock out Poison Ivy and cut her control over the plants. But before Batgirl could act, the shrubs around her pulled back to reveal her hiding place.

"My realm is secure . . . except for one pesky bat," Poison Ivy said with a sneer. "I know you're in there, Batgirl. My plants told me."

Batgirl's element of surprise was gone. She stood up but hid the stun grenade behind her torn cape.

"I've heard about people talking to plants, but I've never heard about the plants talking back," Batgirl said.

The super hero walked calmly toward Poison Ivy. When she was close enough, Batgirl pressed the trigger button on the stun grenade and threw it at the super-villain.

The grenade did not reach its intended target. Poison Ivy gestured and a vine sprouted out of the ground in front of her. In one smooth motion, it snatched the stun grenade from midair.

"I'm very tired of you getting in my way," Poison Ivy said. She made a throwing motion and the vine tossed the stun grenade back at the super hero.

Batgirl rolled out of the way before the grenade exploded.

BWAAAAMM!

The blast knocked over many of the tender vines and flowers as if a storm wind had hit them. The grenade's sound made Batgirl's ears ring, but she was not knocked out. Neither was Poison Ivy.

Suddenly a giant, serpentlike vine sprouted up from the ground in front of Batgirl. The tip of it looked like the head of a snake and it had thorns for fangs. Layers of green leaves covered it like scales. The creature swayed like a cobra before it struck out at her.

Batgirl flipped up and out of the way just in time. Moments later another serpent vine popped up from the ground next to her.

SNAP! SNAP! It tried to grab the super hero with its thorny teeth.

Now Batgirl was caught between two snake vines. She pulled a small canister from her Utility Belt. It had a nozzle on one end. Batgirl aimed it at one of the creatures.

"Ivy, make your monsters back off or I'll be forced to hurt them," Batgirl said.

"With that little thing?" Poison Ivy laughed.

"What's a plant's worst enemy?" Batgirl asked as she put her finger over a button on the side of the canister.

"Humans!" Poison Ivy replied angrily.

"No," Batgirl said. "Fire."

She pressed the button and a flame shot out of the nozzle.

FWOOOOSH!

"Nooo!" Poison Ivy shouted.

"This is a cutting torch," Batgirl said. "I use it to slice through metal, so it will cut through plants very easily."

The snake vines retreated. They sank back into the ground. It looked for a moment as though Poison Ivy was going to accept defeat. But then she smiled.

"You're going to need a bigger torch," Ivy said.

The ground under Batgirl's feet rumbled. Then it heaved as something huge emerged from below. A mythical monster slowly lifted itself out of the ground. It had nine heads made out of snake vines.

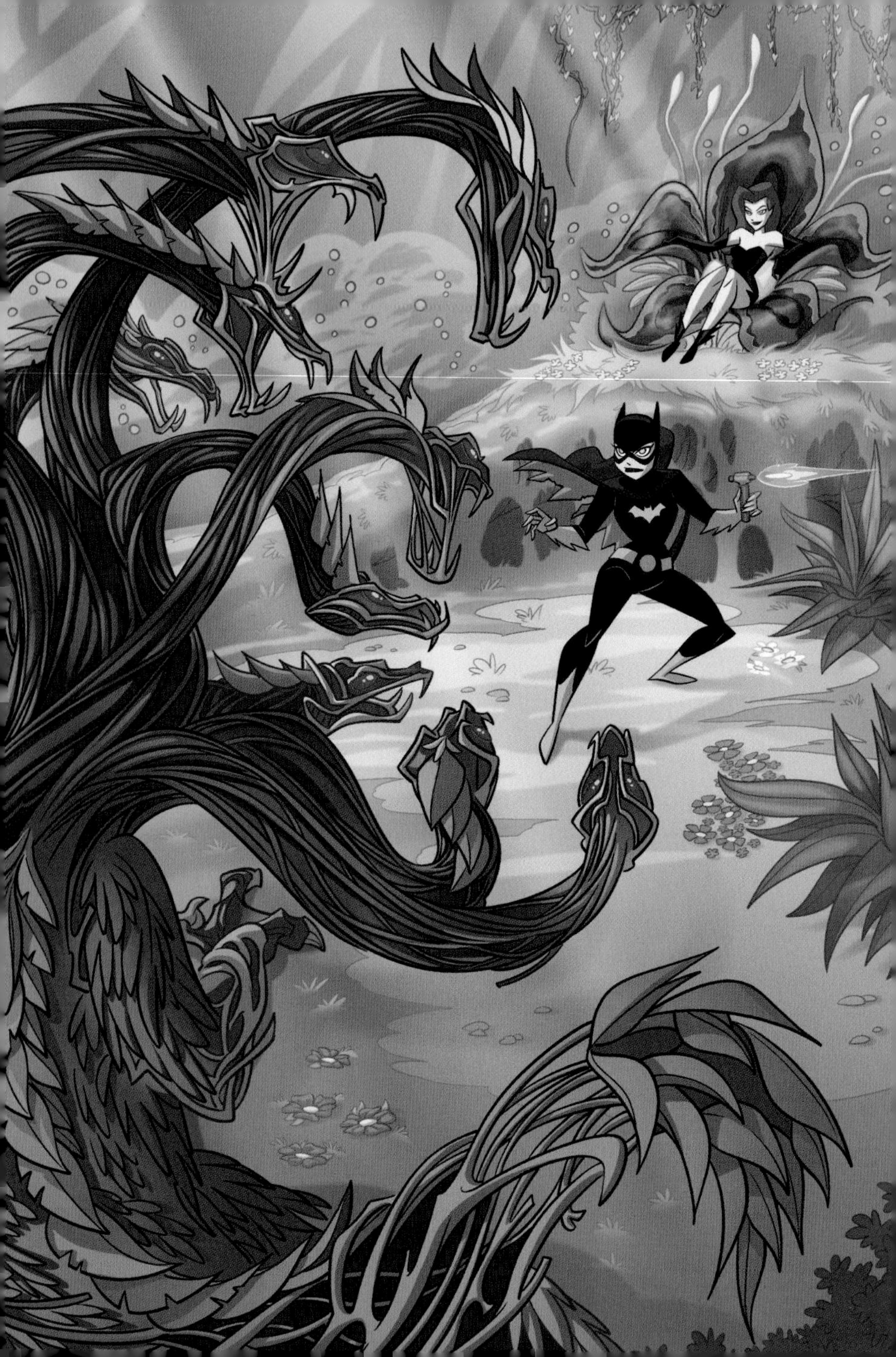

"A Hydra!" Batgirl gasped.

"Yes!" Poison Ivy replied. "And if you destroy one head, it will be replaced with two more. You'll never defeat it."

"Hercules defeated it," Batgirl said. "And so can I!"

The super hero ran toward the monster. She leaped up and swiped the mini cutting torch across one of the serpent vines. It sliced cleanly through the plant like a laser. The head toppled to the ground.

THWUMP!

Batgirl landed on the creature's back. From there she could reach the spot where all the heads grew out of the central body.

SIZZZ! SIZZZ! SIZZZ!

Batgirl quickly sliced through the rest of the snake vines.

But Poison Ivy had told the truth about the heads growing back in twice the number as before. Suddenly new snake vines sprouted from the main Hydra. Where there had been nine heads, now there were eighteen.

Okay, time for Plan B, Batgirl decided.

Poison Ivy laughed in victory as she watched her foe jump off the back of the Hydra monster and run. But the super hero was not retreating. She was giving herself some room to throw a set of special Batarangs.

The villain stopped laughing when she saw each of the Batarangs deploy a net. They dropped down onto the writhing plant creature. The Hydra's heads whipped around and got tangled in the nets. Soon they were completely twisted around themselves and could not move.

"I'm sick and tired of fooling around," Poison Ivy shouted in frustration as she waved her arms. The plant Hydra fell apart just like the T-rex and sank back down into the ground.

"I don't need help defeating you," Poison Ivy declared. "I can do it myself!"

The super-villain threw her arms wide. Thick vines burst from the ground and twisted around her legs. They grew up her body, around her arms, and over her head.

Leaves and flowers of every shape and size covered the twisting tendrils. Poison Ivy was completely encased in her beloved plants within a matter of moments. And then they expanded to gigantic size as Poison Ivy grew an enormous vine body around her own.

"I am the Queen of Green and I will reign supreme!" Poison Ivy shouted.

The towering Ivy monster swiped at Batgirl with a giant hand that was as thick as a tree trunk. The super hero jumped over the hand and grabbed onto one of the flowering vines hanging from Ivy's throne room. She swung from vine to vine as the Ivy monster chased her.

STOMP! STOMP! STOMP! The villain tromped through the lovely garden until all of it was crushed.

"You're not the Queen of Green, you're the Queen of Mulch," Batgirl told Poison Ivy. "Look at what you've done!"

Poison Ivy looked around at the wreckage. The fruit trees were flattened. The flowering vines were torn and all the petals were stripped away. Ivy's throne was a pile of tangled stems and broken twigs.

"Nooo!" Poison Ivy screamed.

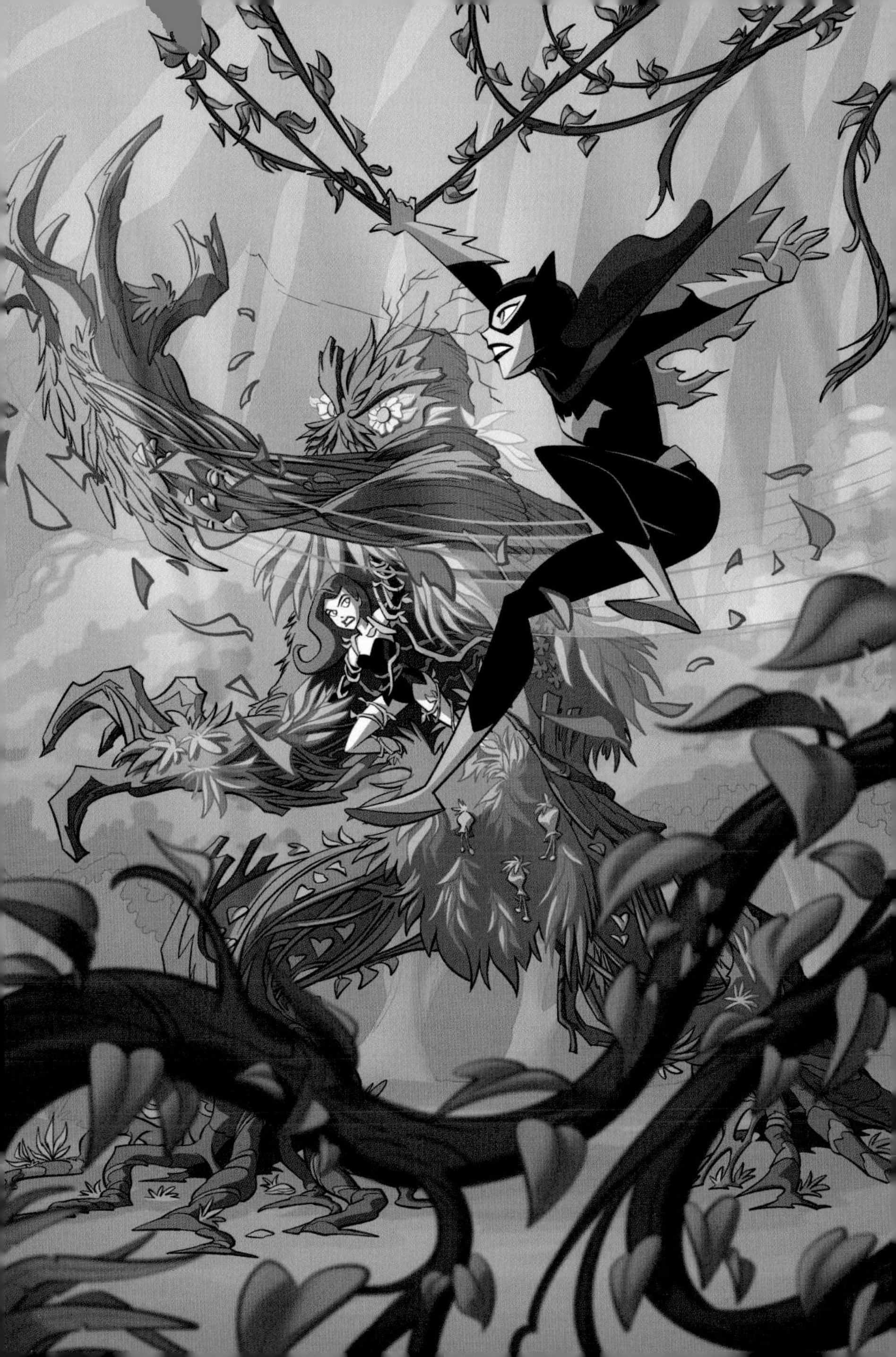

While the super-villain was distracted by the damage she'd caused, Batgirl pulled two capsules from her Utility Belt. She ran up to the giant Ivy monster and crushed the capsules against the vines and leaves. A thin film of frost formed and quickly spread over the plant body that covered Poison Ivy.

"What? What's this?" Ivy said as the frost thickened to ice.

"Freeze capsules," Batgirl replied.

Poison Ivy was trapped inside the Ivy monster as it became encased in ice. The cold quickly knocked her out.

"Pleasant dreams," Batgirl said.

Just as she expected, Poison Ivy's creations started to fall apart once her control was gone. The plant dome over the park began to shrivel and shrink. Bright daylight flooded in.

"Batgirl to Commissioner Gordon," the hero spoke into a small radio handset she kept in her Utility Belt. "You can come and take Poison Ivy away now. But you're going to need a very big police van."

"Thanks, Batgirl!" Gordon replied. "But why would we need a big van?"

"You'll see," Batgirl said.

Batgirl sat down in a warm spot of sunlight and leaned back against a sturdy tree. She picked a wildflower and sniffed its sweet scent.

"This is nice," Batgirl said. "I should come to the park more often."

Poison Ivy

REAL NAME: Pamela Isley

OCCUPATION: Professional Criminal, Botanist

HEIGHT: 5 feet 6 inches

WEIGHT: 110 pounds

EYES: Green

HAIR: Chestnut

POWERS/ABILITIES: Immune to toxins, able to release harmful scents, and capable of controlling plants with her mind. She is also a skilled martial artist and gymnast, making her a tricky foe to capture.

BIOGRAPHY:

Born with immunities to plant toxins and poisons, Pamela Isley's love of plants began to grow like a weed at an early age. She eventually became a botanist, or plant scientist. Through reckless experimentation with various plant life, Pamela Isley's skin itself has become poisonous. Her venomous lips and poisonous plant weapons present a real problem for Batgirl or any other crime-fighter she comes across. But Ivy's most dangerous quality is her extreme love of nature—she cares more about the smallest seedling than any human life.

- Poison Ivy was once engaged to Gotham City's district attorney, Harvey Dent, who eventually became the super-villain Two-Face! Their relationship ended when Dent built a prison on a field of wildflowers, accidentally earning Ivy's wrath.

- Poison Ivy releases toxic scents that can be harmful to humans. Whenever she is locked up in Arkham Asylum, a wall of Plexiglas must separate her from the guards to ensure their safety.

- Ivy's connection to plants is so strong that she can control them by thought alone! The control she has over her lethal plants makes her a dangerous foe for Gotham City Police—as well as Batgirl and the rest of the Batman Family.

BIOGRAPHIES

Author

Laurie S. Sutton has been reading comics since she was a kid. She grew up to become an editor for Marvel, DC Comics, Starblaze, and Tekno Comics. She has written Adam Strange for DC, Star Trek: Voyager for Marvel, plus Star Trek: Deep Space Nine and Witch Hunter for Malibu Comics. There are long boxes of comics in her closet where there should be clothing and shoes. Laurie has lived all over the world and currently resides in Florida.

Illustrator

Leonel Castellani has worked as a comic artist and illustrator for more than twenty years. Mostly known for his work on licensed art for companies such as Warner Bros., DC Comics, Disney, Marvel Entertainment, and Cartoon Network, Leonel has also built a career as a conceptual designer and storyboard artist for video games, movies, and TV. In addition to drawing, Leonel also likes to sculpt and paint. He currently lives in La Plata City, Argentina.

GLOSSARY

allergic (uh-LUR-jik)—having a harmful reaction to something; allergic reactions often include sneezing, swelling, and rashes

catastrophe (kuh-TASS-truh-fee)—a terrible and sudden disaster

corpse flower (KORPS FLOU-ur)—a large flower that smells like a dead body

flora (FLOR-uh)—plant life

grapnel (GRAP-nuhl)—a grappling hook connected to a rope that can be fired like a gun

immune (i-MYOON)—protected from harm

javelin (JAV-uh-luhn)—a light, metal spear that is thrown for distance in a track-and-field event

mulch (MUHLCH)—a material made of decaying leaves and bark that is spread around plants to cover the soil

mutant (MYOO-tuhnt)—a living thing that has developed different characteristics because of a change in its genes

paramedic (pa-ruh-MEH-dik)—a person who treats sick and hurt people before they reach the hospital

pollen (POL-uhn)—a powder made by flowers to help them create new seeds

DISCUSSION QUESTIONS

1. Poison Ivy builds her dome to protect the plants in Gotham City Park. Batgirl thinks Ivy's plan is the wrong way to protect nature. Who do you think is right, and why?

2. Batgirl fails to get inside Ivy's plant dome on her first try. Think of a time you tried something and failed. What did you do next?

3. Poison Ivy creates all kinds of plant creatures in this story. Which one was your favorite? Explain why.

WRITING PROMPTS

1. Batgirl uses a variety of tools from her Utility Belt during her battle with Poison Ivy. Draw a picture of a super hero Utility Belt of your very own. Then make a list of the tools you would carry in it.

2. Poison Ivy has the power to control plants. Imagine that you have that same power. Write a short story about what you would do with that power.

3. Batgirl tells Commissioner Gordon that he will need a big van to take Poison Ivy away. Write a new chapter that explains how the police haul the giant, plant-encased villain away and where they take her.

LOOK FOR MORE

DC SUPER HERO ADVENTURES

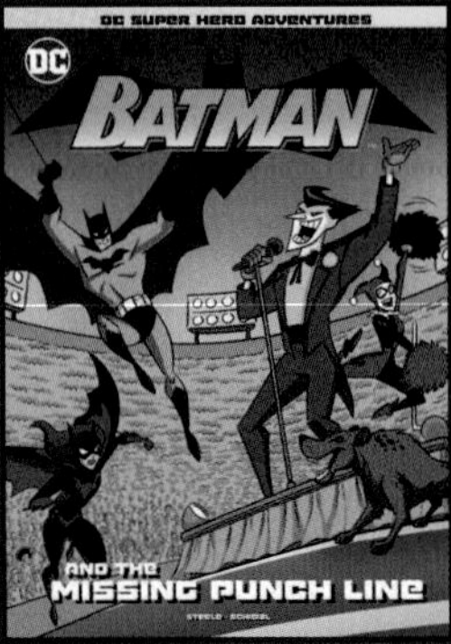
DC SUPER HERO ADVENTURES
DC
BATMAN
AND THE
MISSING PUNCH LINE

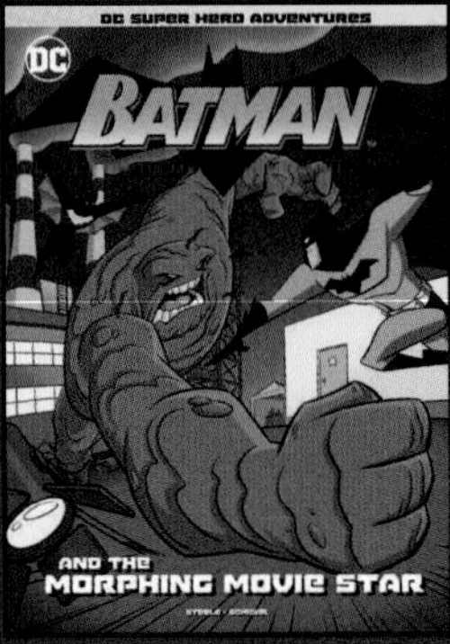
DC SUPER HERO ADVENTURES
DC
BATMAN
AND THE
MORPHING MOVIE STAR

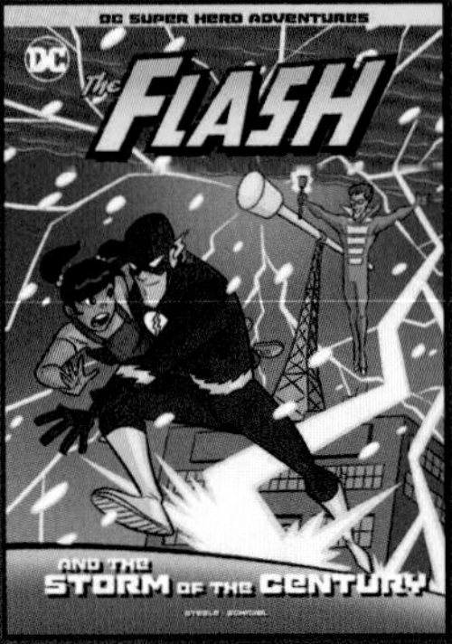
DC SUPER HERO ADVENTURES
DC
The FLASH
AND THE
STORM OF THE CENTURY

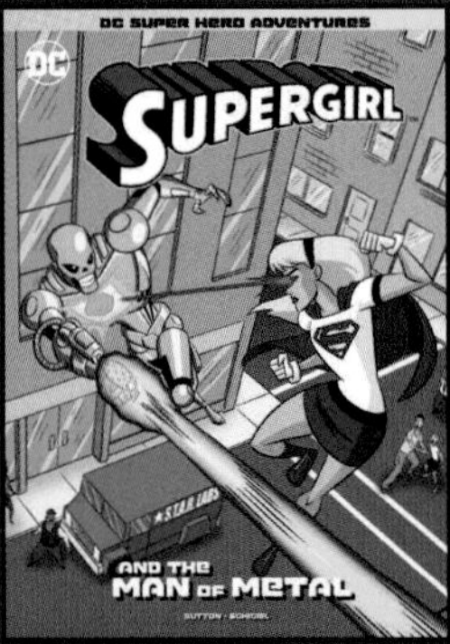
DC SUPER HERO ADVENTURES
DC
SUPERGIRL
AND THE
MAN OF METAL

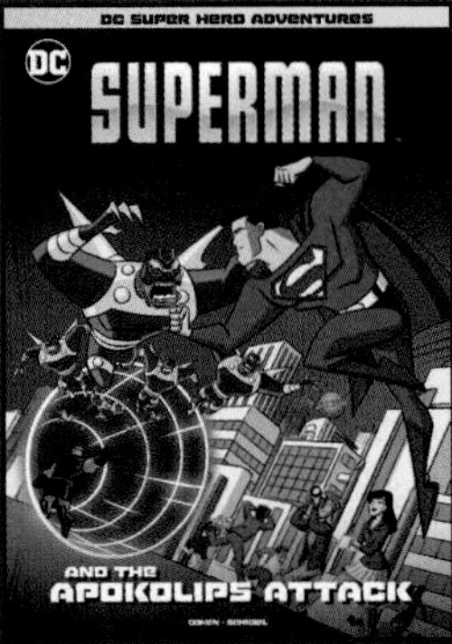
DC SUPER HERO ADVENTURES
DC
SUPERMAN
AND THE
APOKOLIPS ATTACK

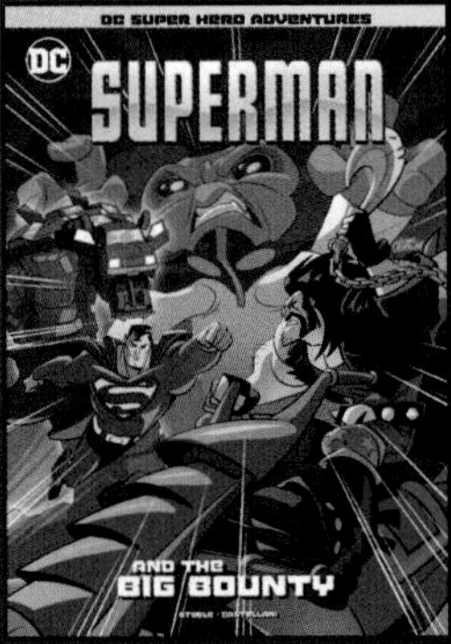
DC SUPER HERO ADVENTURES
DC
SUPERMAN
AND THE
BIG BOUNTY

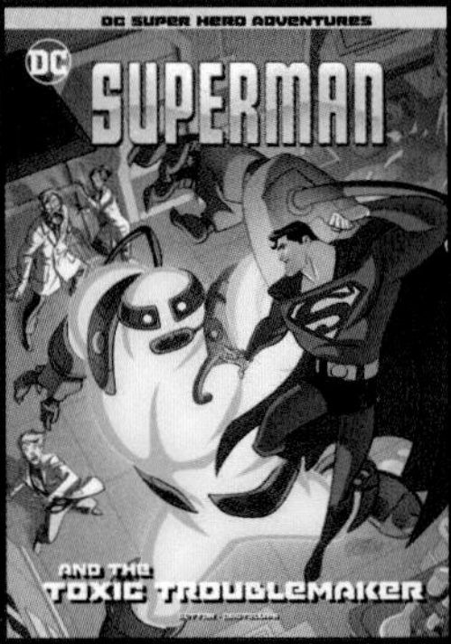
DC SUPER HERO ADVENTURES
DC
SUPERMAN
AND THE
TOXIC TROUBLEMAKER

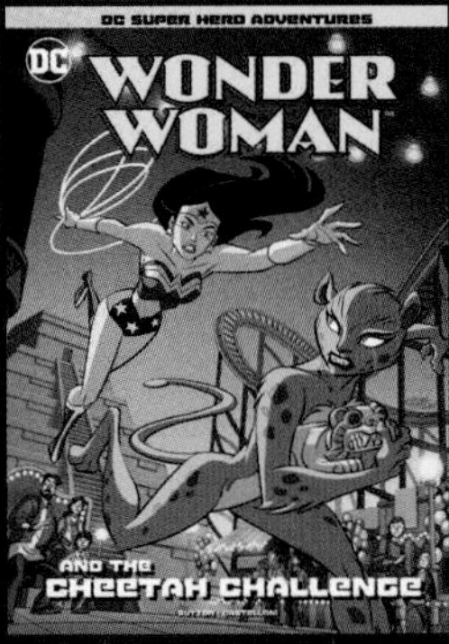
DC SUPER HERO ADVENTURES
DC
WONDER WOMAN
AND THE
CHEETAH CHALLENGE

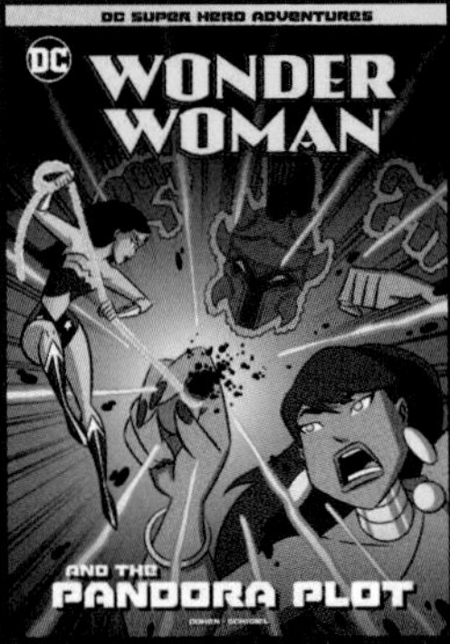
DC SUPER HERO ADVENTURES
DC
WONDER WOMAN
AND THE
PANDORA PLOT